THE CLASSIC
FAIRY TALE COLLECTION

Rapunzel

Retold by JOHN CECH

Illustrated by FIONA SANSOM

STERLING CHILDREN'S BOOKS
New York

WE NEVER REALLY KNOW where a story will begin or end. This one starts with a head of lettuce.

Long ago a man and his wife lived in a tiny house, without a yard, a garden, or even a pot in which to plant tomatoes. Work was scarce, and their stomachs were often empty. Many days they had only a few crusts of old bread to eat, and that was it.

In the garden of the house next to them there were rows and rows of vegetables. "Oh, what I wouldn't give for a handful of those greens," the wife sighed.

She and her husband were expecting their first child. She knew that if she could have just a little of that lettuce, her hunger would be gone and a healthy baby would soon be cooing under their roof. She begged her husband to climb over the garden wall and bring some back.

The man was reluctant to steal—and the owner of the garden was
a woman who was said to have strange and fearsome powers.
Yet his wife looked pale and weak, and he was worried about her health
and that of the baby. So late one night, he climbed over the wall. In a few
moments he scrambled back with a head of fresh lettuce for his sickly
wife. She ate every leaf of it.

The next day, the man's wife wanted another taste of their neighbor's lettuce. She begged her husband to go again, which he did. The next night, she demanded it again. When the man landed on the other side of the wall, their neighbor was waiting. "Ah-ha," she said, "I've found the thief who's been stealing my lettuce."

"I only wanted some for my wife," the man explained. "She is very hungry and is about to have a baby."

"Well, I'll let you have the lettuce," the neighbor said. "But you've got to promise me something in return."

"Anything," the man said. "Anything."

(It's wise to be careful of promises like this because they may be more than you can keep.)

Your wife may have as much lettuce as she would like," said the old woman. "But if I give you the lettuce, you must give your baby to me in return."

The man was shocked. "I couldn't do that!" he cried.

"Would you rather go to jail for stealing?" the neighbor asked. "How would your wife care for your little baby without you?"

So the man agreed. The neighbor would have the couple's first-born child. The old woman was a mighty witch, and the man was afraid that it would be very dangerous to argue with her. His wife was upset and refused to part with her child. Even though it broke his heart, the man could see no other way.

When the woman gave birth to a beautiful little girl, the first
person to appear at their door was the witch from next door.
"Remember your promise?" she asked. The man and his wife wept,
but their tears did not soften the cruel witch. She took the baby with
her deep into the woods, where no one would ever find her.

In the middle of the darkest part of the forest, there is a place without paths or clearings that is lost to everyone. There, the witch had a secret tower without a door and only one window high up at its top. That is where she took the baby.

"I'll call you Rapunzel," she said. "That's the old name for the lettuce your mother loved so much. I'll be your mother now, and you'll be the daughter I never had. I'll keep you safe here in the forest."

So Rapunzel grew up in the tower without any company except for the witch. The witch provided for all of Rapunzel's needs, and the tower was always full of delicious food and pretty clothes. The old woman also brought sacks of wool to the tower, and taught Rapunzel how to spin yarn and to weave the loveliest of tapestries. Rapunzel's hair had never been cut, and its fine golden strands grew so long she could have woven them into her designs. While Rapunzel worked and passed her days in the tower, she sang to herself. She had such a sweet voice that all the birds of the forest came to listen.

Years went by this way, and Rapunzel became a young woman. Her beautiful voice was matched by her beautiful nature. She was kind and gentle, calm and patient. Every day she combed and braided her long, golden hair as she sang to herself. The witch was often gone all day, but in the evenings, she would arrive at the bottom of the tower and call up:

"Rapunzel, my dear, so fair,

send down the ladder of your hair."

Rapunzel would then send the coils of her braid tumbling out the window and down to the ground. The witch would climb up Rapunzel's braid, bringing with her a basket of food for their supper and for the next day.

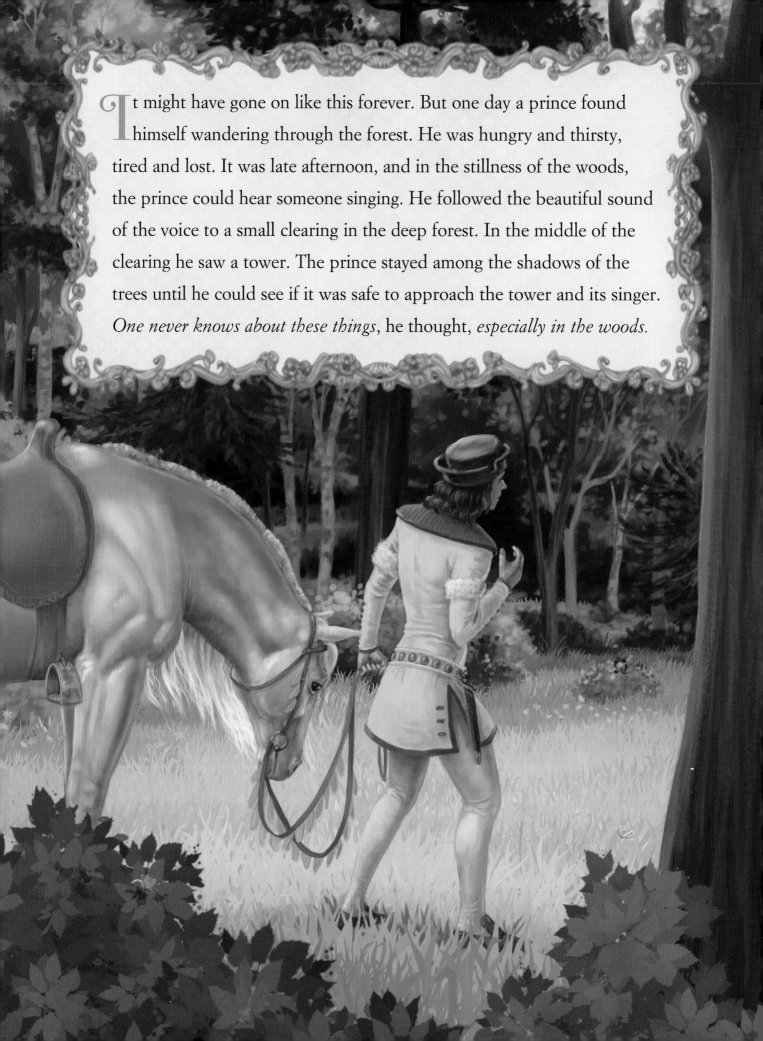

It might have gone on like this forever. But one day a prince found himself wandering through the forest. He was hungry and thirsty, tired and lost. It was late afternoon, and in the stillness of the woods, the prince could hear someone singing. He followed the beautiful sound of the voice to a small clearing in the deep forest. In the middle of the clearing he saw a tower. The prince stayed among the shadows of the trees until he could see if it was safe to approach the tower and its singer. *One never knows about these things*, he thought, *especially in the woods.*

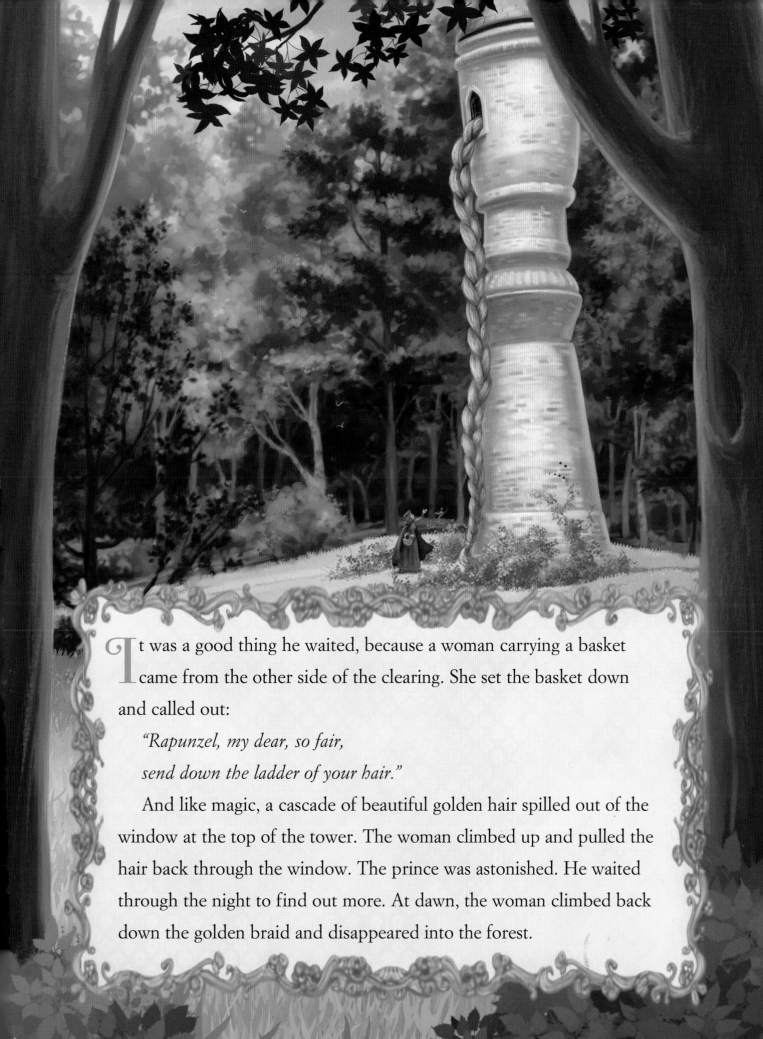

It was a good thing he waited, because a woman carrying a basket came from the other side of the clearing. She set the basket down and called out:

"Rapunzel, my dear, so fair,

send down the ladder of your hair."

And like magic, a cascade of beautiful golden hair spilled out of the window at the top of the tower. The woman climbed up and pulled the hair back through the window. The prince was astonished. He waited through the night to find out more. At dawn, the woman climbed back down the golden braid and disappeared into the forest.

By now the prince was so hungry that he was willing to take
his chances with whomever lived in the tower, and so he called up:

"Rapunzel, my dear, so fair,

send down the ladder of your hair."

The hair spilled down the wall, and the prince climbed up and through
the window at the top of the tower. When the two young people saw
each other, they fell instantly and completely in love. Rapunzel sang to
the prince, shared the food from her basket, and listened to stories of his
kingdom and the wide world beyond that. They were both enthralled, and
the hours passed quickly.

The prince descended from the tower before the witch appeared, and he waited below in the forest until she had left in the morning. Then he climbed back up the braid to Rapunzel. The daily journey up and down Rapunzel's silken hair went on for weeks. And through it all, Rapunzel and the prince never tired of each other's company.

The prince wanted to take Rapunzel away with him, to be his princess and live at the palace.

"My mother will never let me leave," Rapunzel replied sadly. But then she had an idea.

"Each time you visit me, bring a piece of rope. I will hide it and will make a ladder, and we shall escape together."

One morning, as Rapunzel combed out the witch's hair, she sighed. Her thoughts drifted to the prince, and she accidentally said out loud what she had always kept secret: "Oh, I wish you told me stories like the prince does."

"So someone has been visiting you!" The witch was furious and shook her finger at Rapunzel. "How could you have betrayed me when I was keeping you safe from the world?" Now the witch was suspicious. *Could Rapunzel be hiding the prince somewhere?* she thought. Enraged, she searched every inch of the tower and discovered the rope ladder, and she knew that Rapunzel was planning to escape.

The witch picked up a pair of scissors, and with their sharp blades she cut off the young woman's hair. Then, with a few magic words, she whisked Rapunzel from the tower and brought her, in an instant, to a little hut in the middle of a forlorn and empty place far, far away from the forest. There the witch left Rapunzel with the words, "See if your prince will ever find you now!"

The witch returned to the tower. When the prince called for Rapunzel to let down her hair, the witch answered with the braid of Rapunzel's hair that she had kept. When he climbed into the tower, the prince was shocked to see that it was the witch, and not Rapunzel, who was waiting for him. He backed away from the old woman and stumbled out of the tower window. He fell headlong into a patch of thorn bushes beneath the tower. They broke his fall, but he was blinded by their barbs.

ost, and without sight, the prince wandered for years—through ice and snow, over deserts and mountains. He dragged himself along, always hoping to find Rapunzel again. One day he fell into a deep sleep on the hard ground of a lonely valley. He awoke to the sound of singing, and the beautiful voice he heard reminded him of Rapunzel. *Could it be she?* he wondered, *or am I still dreaming?* He found the words and the hope to call out:

"Rapunzel, my dear, so fair,

send down the ladder of your hair."

The singing stopped. Someone was weeping with joy over him, her tears falling on his blinded eyes. Like the wind whisks away clouds, the blindness suddenly vanished. The prince could see again, and he saw that the healing tears came from Rapunzel.

"I thought you must be dead," Rapunzel said.

"I thought I was—until this morning when I heard your song," the prince replied.

The pair shared a warm embrace and reveled in their good fortune of being reunited. Soon they left that desolate valley to return to the prince's land.

When Rapunzel and the prince returned to the kingdom, they were surprised to learn of the rumors the witch was spreading. She boasted far and wide about how she had dealt with an unruly daughter and a meddling prince. It wasn't long before Rapunzel's real mother and father heard the witch's tale, too. They told everyone what really had happened to their daughter.

News of Rapunzel's parents soon reached her and the prince, who invited them for a visit at the palace. The moment she saw them, Rapunzel knew in her heart that they were indeed her real parents. When Rapunzel and the prince were married, Rapunzel's parents came to the wedding. And they stayed on, after the last bite of cake was eaten, to live with the jubilant couple.

And the witch? She packed up her garden and her tower and disappeared. She didn't hear the bells ringing out to celebrate the marriage of Rapunzel and the prince. After so many hardships, the two lived a long and happy life together, full of song, sweet children, and salads.

A Note on the Story

The most familiar version of "Rapunzel" appeared in 1812, in the now-famous collection from the Brothers Grimm, *The Household Tales*. But the Grimms built the story they published on a basic plot that had appeared hundreds of years earlier. Perhaps the best known relative of the Rapunzel story is "Petrosinella," which made its debut in Giambattista Basile's collection of Italian folktales, the *Pentamerone* (1637). Petrosinella is the Italian name for parsley, and in Basile's tale, an expectant mother has a craving for this herb. Her unrestrained appetite leads her to an ogress's forbidden garden, where she steals the plant, and must ultimately pay for her crime by giving up her daughter. The girl is raised by the ogress in a tower, and she meets a wandering prince, just as the title character does in "Rapunzel." Together they escape, using the ogress's own magic against her, and they live happily ever after.

A French version of the story, "Persinette," written in the middle of the eighteenth century by Charlotte-Rose de Caumont La Force, also appeared before the Grimms' tale. Here, the parsley is found in the garden of a fairy, who demands the child in repayment for the father's crime of stealing the herb for his pregnant wife. Persinette is sequestered in a luxurious tower by the fairy, but eventually she and the prince meet. The two are parted when the fairy discovers them—the prince is blinded and Persinette is exiled. When they find each other again, the prince's eyesight is restored. In the end, the fairy is overwhelmed with compassion for the couple and returns them to the prince's palace.

There are a good number of variations on the "Rapunzel" story, including other versions from Italy and France, as well as similar tales from Greece, Egypt, and even the Kentucky mountains, where the father's theft is a head of cabbage, and the girl is named Reptensil. The heroine in this down-home version ends up saving the prince by tricking the witch into running off a cliff to her demise. Most recently, parts of the "Rapunzel" story were woven into Stephen Sondheim's 1986 musical, *Into the Woods*.

Where would a story like "Rapunzel" come from? One of the ancient and persistent themes of the story is the desire of parents to keep their daughters secluded so that they are protected from the world and from any possible romances prior to marriage. One of the early threads of this tale is perhaps to be found in the story of Saint Barbara, whose father locked her in a tower to protect her virtue. She didn't actually meet a prince, but while her father was traveling on business, she converted to Christianity and was eventually martyred for her beliefs.

Another thread of the story is the folklore concerning the often stereotyped cravings of expectant women. In some societies it was (and still is) thought that to preserve the safe delivery of a baby and the health of the mother, the mother's cravings for particular foods should be honored and satisfied. Beyond being old wives' tales, these attitudes may reflect a real nutritional truth. The longing for rapunzel, rampion, or parsley may signal an urge to remedy a vitamin deficiency with iron-rich vegetables like these.

—J. C.